Tsunami

Contents

Introduction

Imagine a pleasant early morning on a tropical island. You are travelling by bus on your way to school. Suddenly, the bus lurches from side to side, the ride becomes bumpy and the ground shakes violently. The people around you scream in fear. There is chaos and panic. Then, someone points to the ocean. You turn around with a hollow feeling in the pit of your stomach. You catch your breath. A wall of water is approaching the shore.

This happened in the Samoan islands on 29 September 2009. A strong undersea earthquake occurred some 196 kilometres south of Apia, the

People search in the wreckage left by the tsunami in Samoa.

capital of Samoa, at just before 7.00 A.M. Samoan time. The earthquake started four enormous and deadly waves, or tsunami, that struck the coasts of Samoa, American Samoa and Tonga. The giant waves were almost 6 metres tall. They washed almost 2 kilometres inland in some areas where they struck. The Samoan people had almost no time to react to warnings that a series of giant waves were on the way. The first wave reached land around 15 minutes after the earthquake happened.

The bus driver stayed calm. He raced the bus to the top of a nearby hill. This saved the lives of his passengers. However, nearly 200 people died in this tragic natural disaster. Thousands more lost their homes and all their possessions.

What Is a Tsunami?

Powerful, enormous and deadly waves that form in the ocean are called tsunami. A tsunami starts when an event, such as an earthquake, happens in the ocean that forces a large amount of water from one place to another. The force that pushes the water away is a form of energy. It sends shock waves rippling from the point on Earth's surface directly above the place where the earthquake began, or **epicentre**.

The water that is forced away forms the tsunami, or a series of waves called a **wave train**. Tsunami and wave trains can start out small, but they can become very dangerous. When tsunami and wave trains start, nothing can stop them. They can travel across an entire ocean in just one day. The force keeps on pushing the water ahead of it until all the energy in the force is used up.

Tsunami may travel for thousands of kilometres in deep water without being noticed. They may even travel unnoticed beneath a ship out at sea. It is only near land, where the water is shallower, that the wave gets taller.

Sometimes, the energy of the force gets used up before the tsunami strikes land. Tsunami that do reach land can have a weak or strong force behind them. The force behind a tsunami can be so strong as it strikes land that many people drown. A tsunami can wash away animals, buildings and everything else in its path.

Scientists can track a tsunami and tell ahead of time, or **predict**, when a tsunami is about to strike land. They can warn people who are in danger. However, the waves often reach land so fast that people do not have enough time to get to a safe, high place away from the shore.

How a Tsunami Forms and Moves

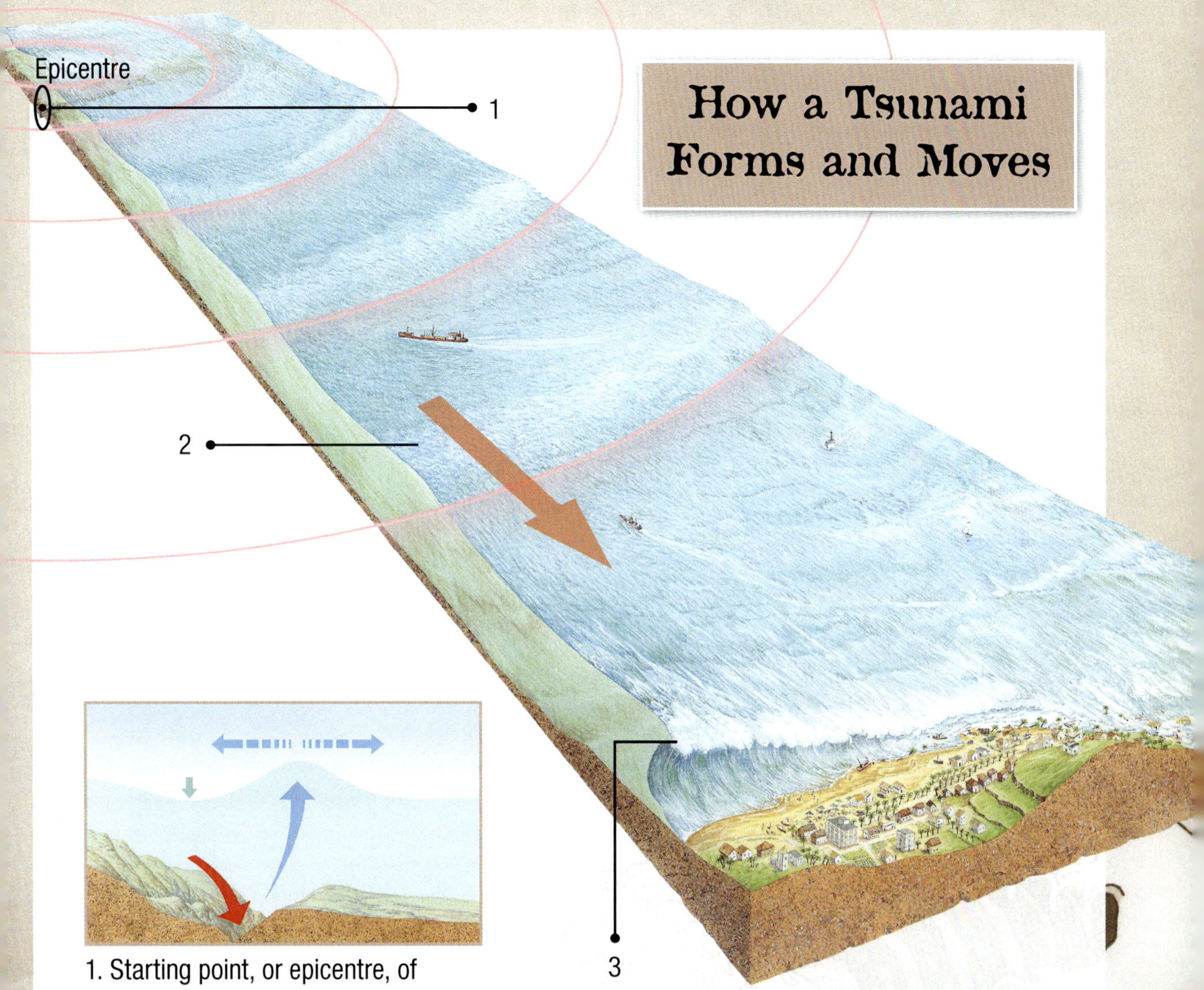

1. Starting point, or epicentre, of a catastrophic event, such as an earthquake, shown here.

2. Shallow waves move quickly. They may go unnoticed.

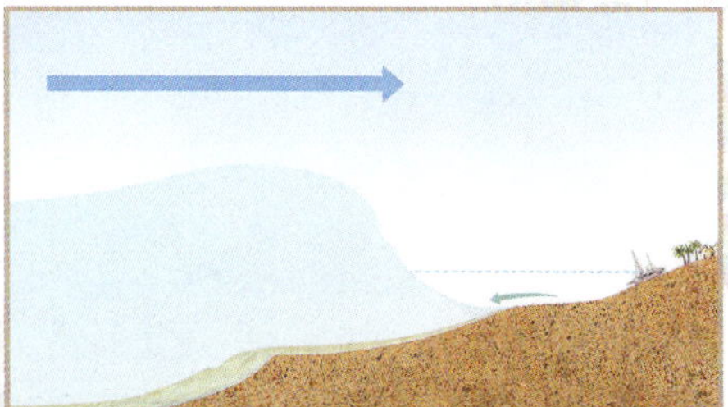

3. As the waves hit shallow waters, they slow down, but become much taller.

The Ocean in Motion

An ocean is always in motion. Currents flow and swirl. Tides rise and fall. Waves race into the shore. Most waves are formed by the wind blowing across the surface of the ocean. But a tsunami is very different from wind waves. The energy driving a tsunami comes from events that happen suddenly under water. It can come from an earthquake or a volcanic eruption under the sea. It can also come from a flying chunk of space rock, called a meteor, falling into the ocean and crashing into the sea floor. Forces from inside Earth, released through undersea earthquakes that send out waves of energy called **seismic energy**, start the majority of tsunami. Seismic energy from an earthquake started the tsunami in Samoa in 2009.

Wind waves break on the shoreline.

There are several ways in which wind waves differ from tsunami.

- Wind waves travel more slowly than tsunami. Tsunami can travel at speeds of up to 965 kilometres per hour. That is as fast as a jet plane.
- Wind waves are much shorter than tsunami when they strike land. The biggest tsunami can reach the height of a 10-storey building.
- The distance between wind waves, or sets of wind waves, is short, but the distance between tsunami can be very long. A wave train can sometimes stretch over hundreds of kilometres.
- Wind waves build up to a steep front that usually breaks against land, but most tsunami waves are not breakers. They simply keep flowing inland to flood coastal and low-lying areas.

Wind Waves and Tsunami

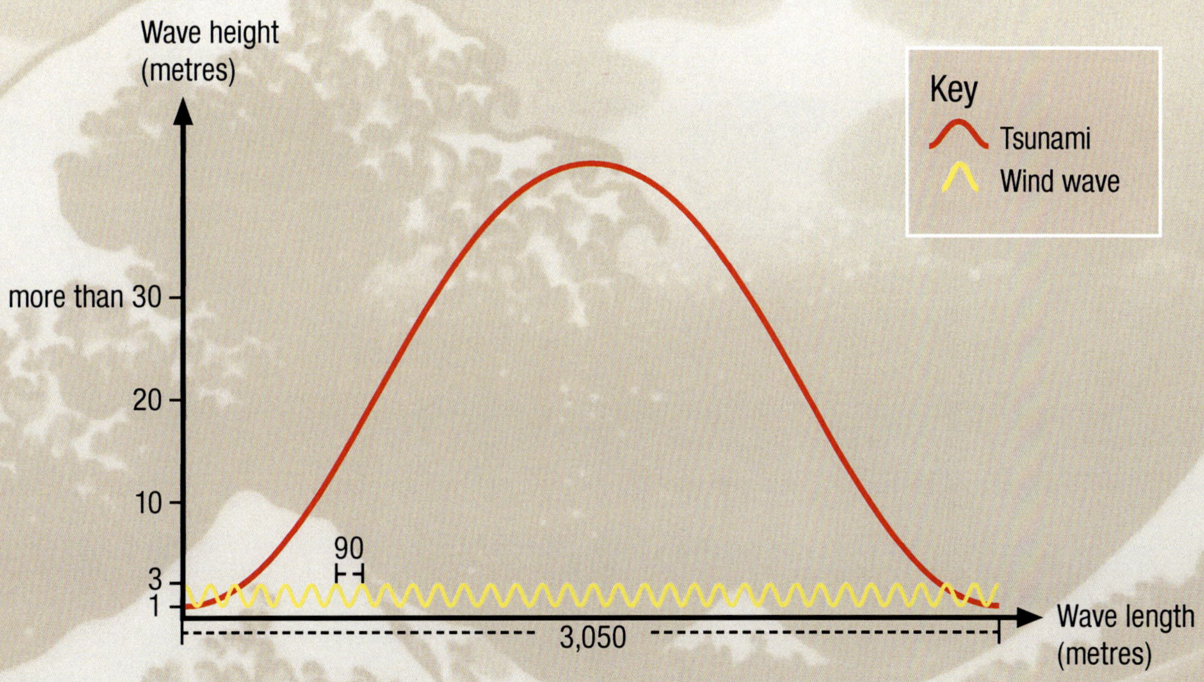

The Source of the Force

The seismic energy that started the tsunami that caused so much sorrow and loss in Samoa came from deep inside Earth. This energy travelled to Samoa through a number of steps.

The energy started as heat energy deep within the centre of Earth. Scientists have learned that Earth consists of four main layers. At the very heart of the planet, there is a centre made mostly of solid, hot iron called the **inner core**. The inner core is extremely hot. Scientists believe that the temperature of Earth's inner core is as high as 7,000 degrees Celsius.

Around the inner core is a layer of boiling, liquid iron called the **outer core**. Heat energy moves from Earth's solid inner core to its outer core. The heat energy makes the outer core boil. It bubbles and flows. The boiling mixture moves around in currents. Scientists believe the temperature of the outer core ranges from 3,700 to 4,300 degrees Celsius.

Between the outer core and Earth's surface is a thick layer of hot, partly melted rock that flows in currents. This layer is the **mantle**. The mantle is cooler than the outer core but still very hot. The hot rock in the lower part of the mantle flows upwards slowly, while the cooler rock in the upper part of the mantle, directly beneath Earth's rocky surface layer, sinks. Currents from the outer core move through the mantle and cause the mantle's surface to shift around and change shape.

When Earth's surface breaks, as when a volcano erupts, you can see the melted rock underneath it.

The outermost, solid layer of Earth that we see and touch is called the **crust**. The crust floats on the surface of the mantle. Earth's crust is between 8 and 40 kilometres thick, although it can be thicker in some places. It is thinnest below the sea and thickest beneath the continents. It consists of cool, rigid rock. However, the rock that forms the sea floor, or oceanic crust, is different from the rock that forms dry land, or **terrestrial crust**. Oceanic crust is thinner but heavier than terrestrial crust.

Earth's Layers

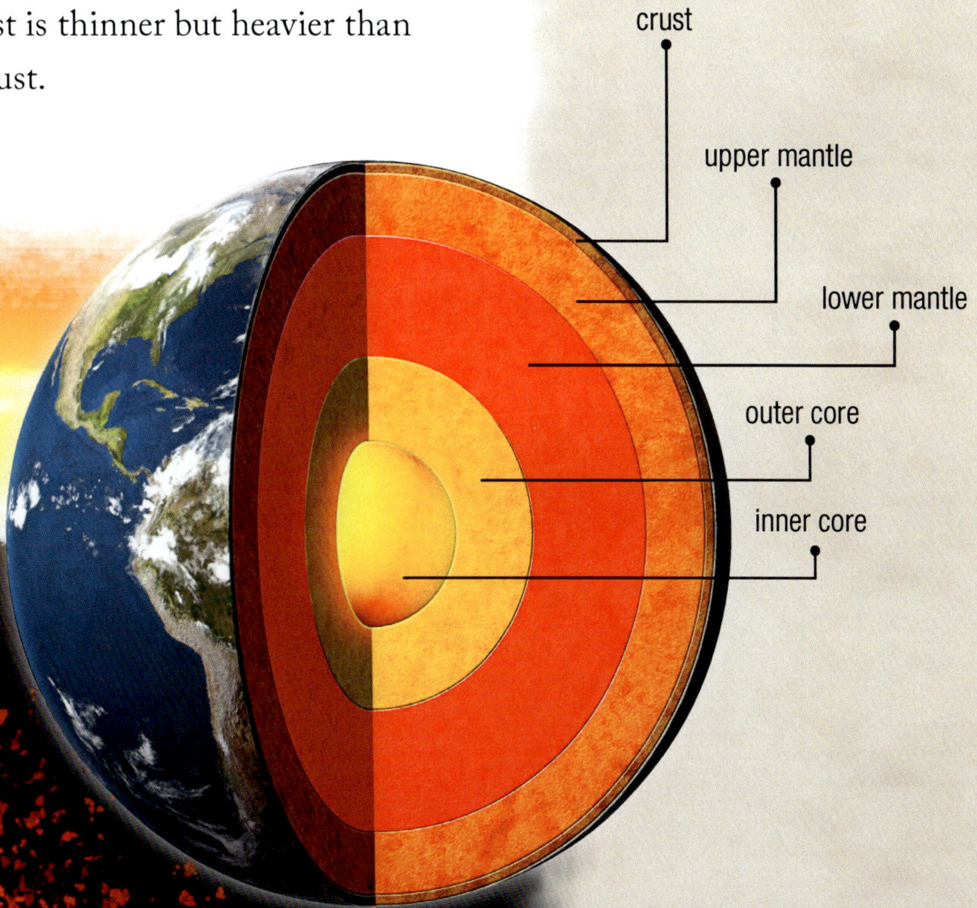

When Plates Collide

Mount St. Helens erupts in the USA in 1980.

As the surface of the mantle moves and bulges, it shifts Earth's terrestrial crust around, too. However, Earth's crust is not one solid, unbroken slab of rock. It is divided into several big and smaller slabs of rock, called **tectonic plates**. The tectonic plates vary in size and shape. Their edges, or boundaries, fit snugly together. The boundaries of the plates cut randomly through oceans and continents.

Tectonic plates are always on the move. However, the plates do not move at the same speed or in the same direction. Sometimes, plates pull away from each other. Sometimes, their edges grind against each other. Sometimes, they move towards each other and collide.

Most earthquakes and volcanoes occur along the edges where tectonic plates meet and move. When two plate edges grind over each other or move towards each other and collide, their energy makes the ground shake. People feel this energy as earth tremors or earthquakes. Seismic energy can cause trees to fall and buildings to collapse. It can make huge rifts in the ground.

When an earthquake happens underwater, something else happens, too. The seismic energy shifts ocean water from one place to another. Sometimes, it is strong enough to shove a large amount of ocean water far enough to flood land. This is what happened in Samoa.

The area around the edge of the Pacific Plate is called the Pacific Ring of Fire, as so much seismic activity happens here. Samoa sits on the edge of the Pacific Plate, close to where it meets the Australian Plate. The two plates collide and press together with a lot of force. Sometimes, they get stuck and cannot move freely anymore. Seismic energy builds up. At some point, the built-up energy breaks free. Nobody knows how long the seismic energy from the Samoa earthquake had been building up. Scientists do know that there was enough energy for a 300-kilometre stretch of sea floor to suddenly shift up around 7 metres.

Samoa and the Pacific Plate

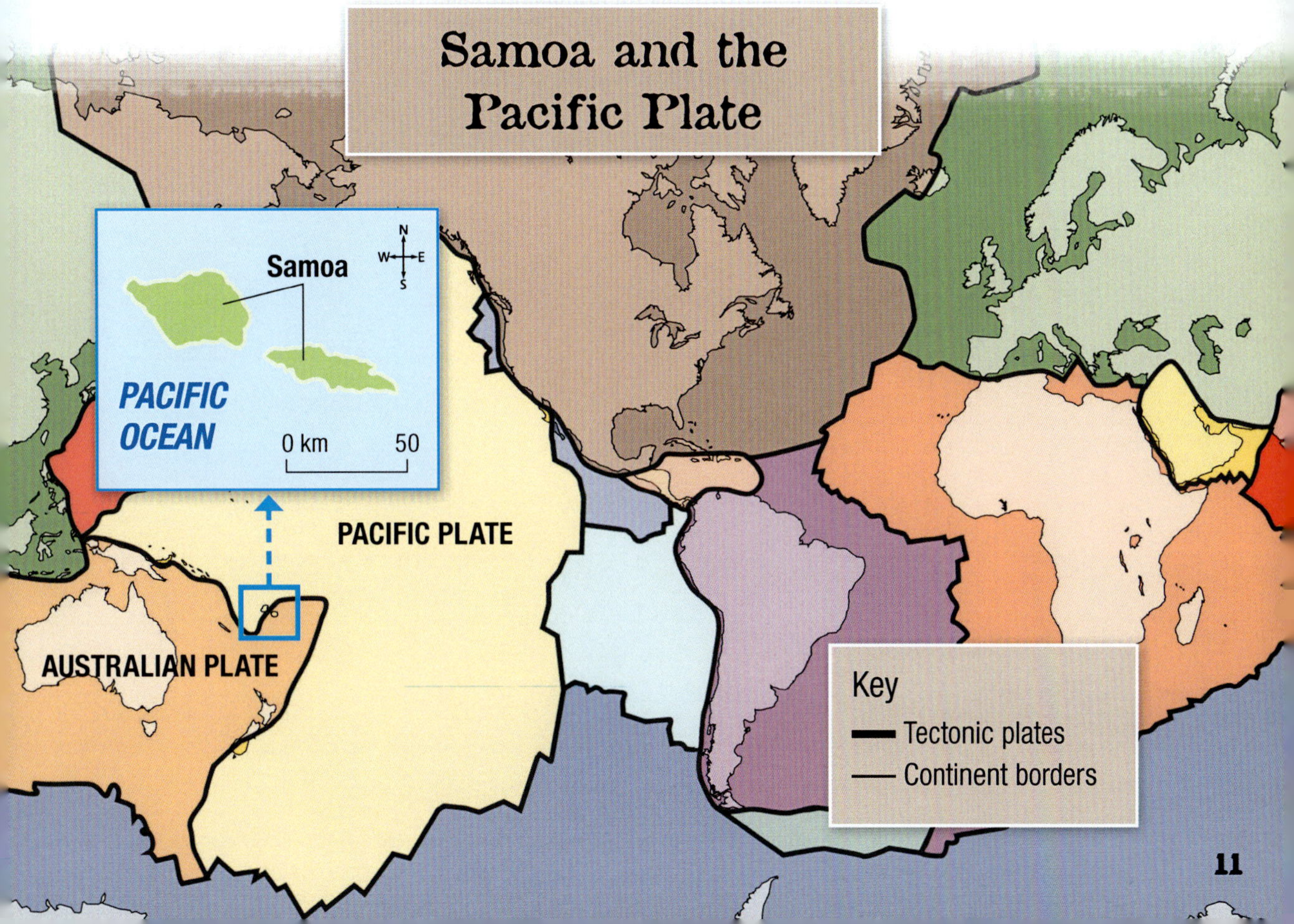

Waves and Water Walls

When an earthquake happens underwater, people on land may or may not feel the tremors. In the ocean, the movement of the plate gives the water overlying it an enormous upward shove. The plate movement also often shoots rocks up into the water with tremendous force. These rocks shove the water upwards even more.

Next, the water that was shoved away forms a wave directly above the epicentre of the earthquake. The seismic energy moves away from the epicentre of the earthquake in all directions. It drives the water that was disturbed ahead of it. The epicentre is where a tsunami wave begins.

The distance the tsunami wave travels and the obstacles it meets, such as coral reefs and land, use up the energy that drives it. Eventually, all the seismic energy will be used up. Sometimes, this happens before the tsunami reaches land. However, sometimes, the force driving a tsunami is so powerful that the wave reaches shore as a vertical wall of water and causes great damage on land.

This picture shows what a tsunami might look like in a big city. It is not a real photograph.

A tsunami that still has a lot of force behind it when it reaches the shoreline will raise the level of the ocean to a point that is much higher than its normal level. Wind energy may further increase the height of the tsunami. All of these factors determine the damage the wave will do on land.

The energy the wave spends on land can be measured. One way is to measure how far the tsunami washes inland. Another is to measure how much higher than normal the sea level was. The areas of greatest risk during a tsunami strike are within 2 kilometres of the shoreline and below 15 metres above sea level. These areas are more likely to be affected by the destructive power behind forceful waves. Sadly, a tsunami's destructive power can be measured in terms of human suffering, too. Tsunami often result in staggering death counts. This is especially true if people have little or no warning.

A coastal town in Indonesia lies destroyed after a tsunami.

Striking Land

Over the centuries, many tsunami have struck harbours in Japan, which lies on the edge of the Pacific Plate. *Tsunami* is a Japanese word that means *great harbour wave*. Different factors influence how a great harbour wave will strike land. One depends on whether the land lies on the side of the lighter terrestrial crust or if it lies on the side of the heavier oceanic crust. The features of the sea floor and the features of the shoreline also play a part.

In the first instance, a tsunami can strike land with its crest first, or with its trough first. If the land is on the side of the lighter, higher plate, the tsunami's crest will reach land first. If the land is on the side of the heavier, lower plate the wave's trough will reach land first. When this happens, a dramatic event occurs when the first tsunami is about halfway on its journey to the shore. The water suddenly pulls back from the shore. This sometimes exposes huge areas of beach and seabed that are usually under the sea. This event is called drawback. It can be a vital warning to people that a tsunami is on the way.

The Samoan and Tongan communities saw a drawback on their shorelines before the tsunami hit. Some people were unaware of the danger and wandered into the exposed seabed area. This cost them their lives when the first tsunami struck soon after.

In the second instance, the features of the seabed and shoreline influence the tsunami's strength. When a tsunami wave travels into a bay with a wide entrance and the bay then becomes narrower or enclosed, the wave will grow taller.

If the sea floor leading to the shoreline becomes very shallow very suddenly, the deep water before it can shape a tsunami wave into a giant, steep wave with a breaking front. On the other hand, a coral reef close to shore will absorb a lot of the tsunami wave's energy. This can reduce its impact on the land. Trees on the shoreline can also absorb a tsunami wave's energy.

Water Drawback before a Tsunami Strike

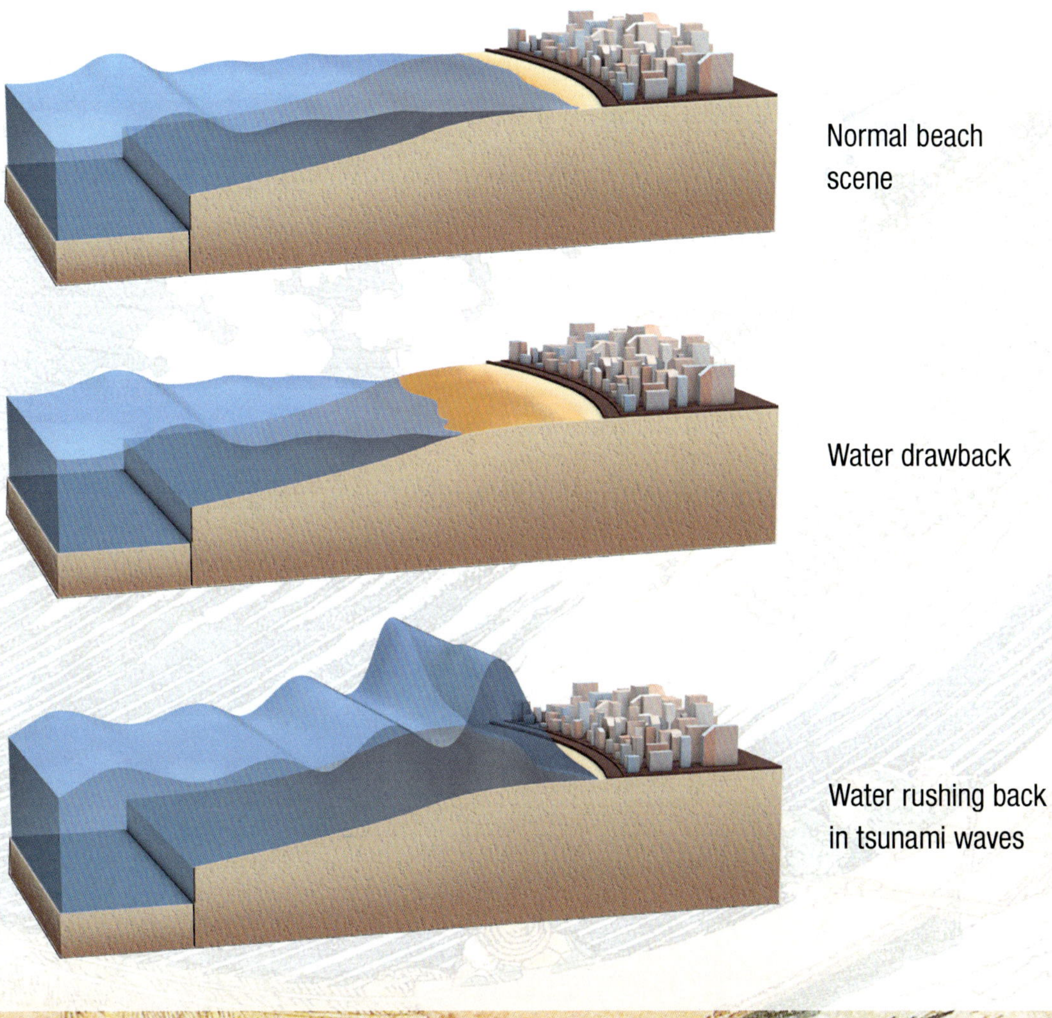

Tracking a Tsunami

A tsunami hazard zone sign in Thailand

A large tsunami has a terrible impact on everyday life in the affected community. Families must cope with the loss of loved ones. Some families lose everything they have, including their homes. Public services in the affected area may stop working. Also, as is the case after any natural disaster in a populated area, crime can become a problem until authorities are able to restore order.

In some places today, early-warning systems are making it easier for scientists to predict when and where a tsunami might hit. With warning systems in place, governments are better able to warn people when a tsunami is on the way. Countries in and around the Pacific Ocean are most at risk of tsunami, but all coastal states have a tsunami risk. Only some have warning stations. However, world leaders recently agreed to work together and share information about underwater earthquakes and tsunami.

Two large warning centres work together to track tsunami in the Pacific Ocean. They are the Pacific Tsunami Warning Center in Hawaii and the West Coast and Alaska Tsunami Warning Center in Alaska.

Pacific Ocean

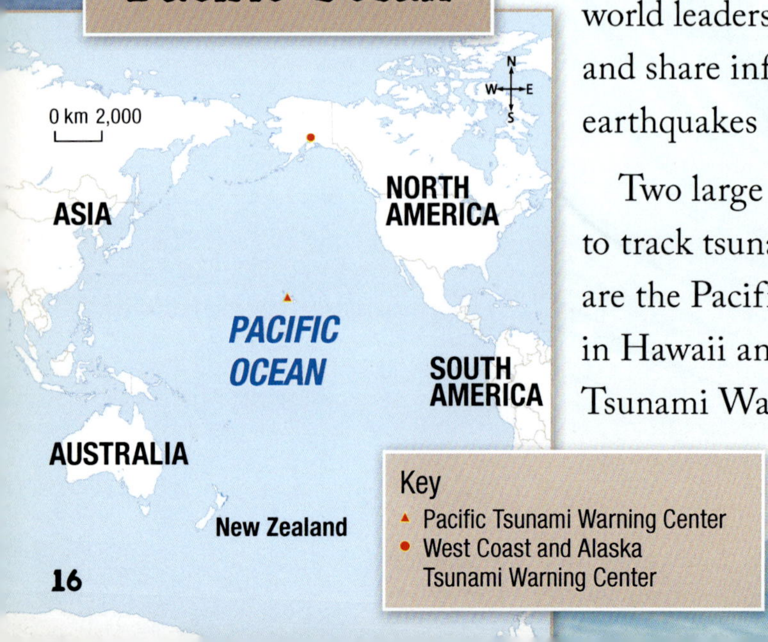

Scientists at work at India's Tsunami Warning Centre

Scientists at tsunami warning centres use special equipment to gather information about a possible tsunami. They record earthquake activity and measure changes in sea level far out in the open ocean. The equipment reports the information to tsunami warning centre computers. Scientists use the computers to help them process the information. They can then predict whether a tsunami will strike land. They can also predict its expected wave height and arrival time.

The centres warn countries when they believe a tsunami is on its way. They also let the media know. People can then learn about it from radio and television reports. However, it is a government's responsibility to make sure its people know about incoming tsunami and how to keep safe. The government must put emergency plans in place to move people to safe places before a tsunami strikes land. The government must also plan how to manage the situation after the tsunami strikes.

After the Wave

An estimated 192 people died as a result of the tsunami that struck Samoa. The Pacific Tsunami Warning Center in Hawaii issued a tsunami warning. Local authorities blew sirens to announce the approaching tsunami. However, the waves reached the islands so quickly, residents had only minutes to respond. Many could not leave dangerous areas in time. Some people were swept out to sea. The bodies of others were later found wedged in mud and in swamps.

Entire villages were destroyed. Thousands of people became homeless. Battered property, such as boats, cars and household items, lay along the coastline. People's possessions were washed away into the open ocean. The authorities had to put up shelters to house people who had lost their homes. The authorities had to provide many people with clean water, food and health care, too.

Electricity stopped working in some areas for weeks. Communication lines were down. This made emergency work difficult. It made it difficult to count how many people had died, how much damage had been done and where help was needed. Many of the dead had to be taken to temporary morgues on the backs of open trucks. A special medical team helped identify the bodies. They helped find relatives to tell them the sad news.

Work crews inspect damage from a tsunami.

Governments and aid organisations from around the world did their best to help the people of Samoa and Tonga. They sent building materials, clothes, food, medicine, money and volunteer workers to the area. They rebuilt homes, provided medical care and restored the supply of fresh drinking water to the region.

After a tsunami, the ocean eventually settles down again. All the water that came onto land retreats back into the ocean. Plants grow back. People build new houses. However, the people who lived through it never forget such a terrible tragedy.

Girls play in a tent at the camp set up for survivors of the Samoan tsunami.

Conclusion

As is the case with any natural disaster, a tsunami reminds us of how powerless we are before the awe-inspiring forces of nature. The best, most modern technology cannot always prevent deaths during such an event. It also reminds us once more that all the people on Earth are members of one big family. In the aftermath of a natural disaster, such as a tsunami, the kindness of people from around the world towards others in need is often almost beyond belief. No matter how far away we are from the disaster-struck region, each and every one of us can offer help in some small way.

Soldiers pack food for survivors of the tsunami in Indonesia.

Glossary

crust – the solid, surface layer of Earth

epicentre – the point that is directly above the starting place of an earthquake

inner core – an extremely hot mass of solid iron in the centre of Earth

mantle – the thick layer between Earth's crust and the outer core

outer core – a layer of boiling, liquid iron surrounding the inner core

predict – to say what might happen in the future, based on best evidence

seismic energy – to do with an earthquake or a tremor

tectonic plates – rigid slabs of Earth's rocky crust that float and move on the mantle

terrestrial crust – to do with the land on Earth

wave train – a series of tsunami waves

Index

Activities

Genre Focus

Explanation

An explanation is a text that explains how or why things occur, work or are performed.

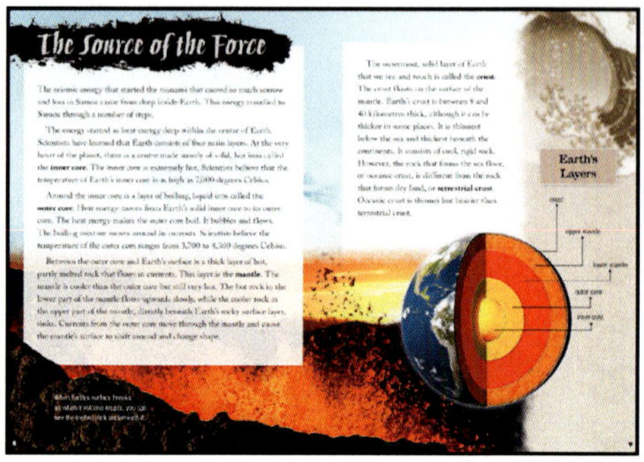

Looking back at an EXPLANATION

The text you have just read explains what a tsunami is, how it is formed and how it can impact upon land and, subsequently, human life.

1. Reading the introduction, what three facts did you learn about the Samoan tsunami?

2. On page 7, the author explains how tsunami and wind waves differ. Complete the graphic organiser below to show how the waves differ.

	Tsunami waves	Wind waves
Speed of waves		
Height of waves		
Distance between waves		
Impact of land on the waves		

3. Use the text on page 14 to help you explain what happens when the trough of a tsunami wave hits land before the crest.

4. Complete a diagram like this one to show the effects of the 2009 Samoan tsunami. Include as many boxes as you need.

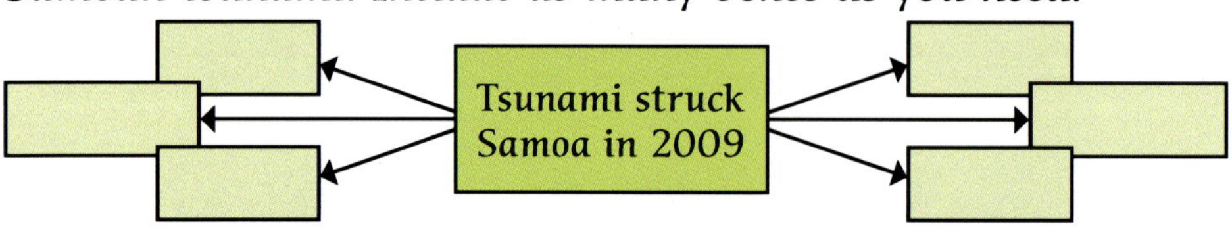

5. What is the main idea of the conclusion on page 20 of the text?

Writing an Explanation

The power of nature has caused many great disasters throughout history. Choose, research and take notes on one of these: volcanic eruptions, earthquakes, floods or hurricanes. Use your notes to write an explanation.

1. The first thing you need to do is write an introduction. This need only be a couple of sentences that inform the reader of what is to be explained.
2. Now, with the support of labelled diagrams, write about what causes the force of nature you have chosen. Your explanation of the process needs to include the presentation of ordered stages. To do this you can use time connectives such as first, then, next and finally or you can number the stages.
3. You could include an example of the natural force you have chosen, for example the Icelandic volcano in 2010, Hurricane Katrina in 2005 or the Maitland Floods of 2007. Keep this section explanatory by telling what led to the disaster and the immediate and later impact it had.
4. Write a conclusion to your text. This could relate to the power nature can have over humans, methods that have been put in place to lessen the impact of such natural phenomena or what people can do to help others affected by disasters.
5. Re-read your text to check the structure, content, grammar and spelling.

Comprehension Focus

Cause and Effect, Figurative Language

Remember

Cause and effect is the relationship between what happens and why it happens.
Figurative language is the use of figures of speech such as metaphors, similes, idioms and onomatopoeia, to build up images.

1. Draw up and complete a diagram similar to the one below to show causes and effects of the following natural disasters.

CAUSE	EFFECTS
Volcanic eruption	
Earthquake	
Flood	

2. Create your own figures of speech that could be used to build up images about the following natural disasters.

Bushfire			
Simile	Onomatopoeia	Metaphor	Alliteration
Drought			
Simile	Onomatopoeia	Metaphor	Alliteration
Tsunami			
Simile	Onomatopoeia	Metaphor	Alliteration